DATE DUE

Southeast Asia

SOUTHEAST ASIA

country	area square miles (sq km)	population (1991)	capital	currency
BRUNEI DARUSSALAM	2,226 (5,800)	300,000	BANDAR SERI BEGAWAN	Brunei dollar
CAMBODIA	69,898 (181,000)	8.6 million	PHNOM PENH	Riel
INDONESIA	578,173 (1,497,461)	187.7 million	JAKARTA	Rupiah
LAOS	91,430 (236,800)	4.3 million	VIENTIANE	Kip
MALAYSIA	127,317 (329,749)	18.4 million	KUALA LUMPUR	Ringgit
MYANMAR (BURMA)	261,218 (676,552)	42.7 million	YANGON (RANGOON)	Kyat
PHILIPPINES	116,000 (300,000)	63.8 million	MANILA	Peso
SINGAPORE	239 (620)	2.7 million	SINGAPORE	Singapore dollar
THAILAND	198,500 (514,000)	55.4 million	BANGKOK	Baht
VIETNAM	127,242 (329,556)	68.1 million	HANOI	Dong

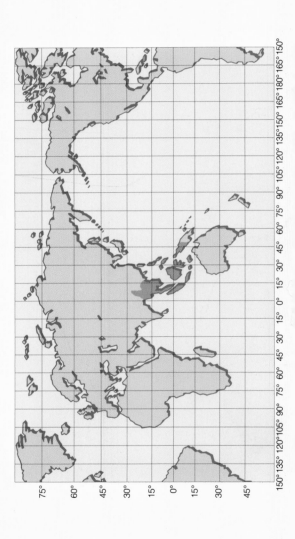

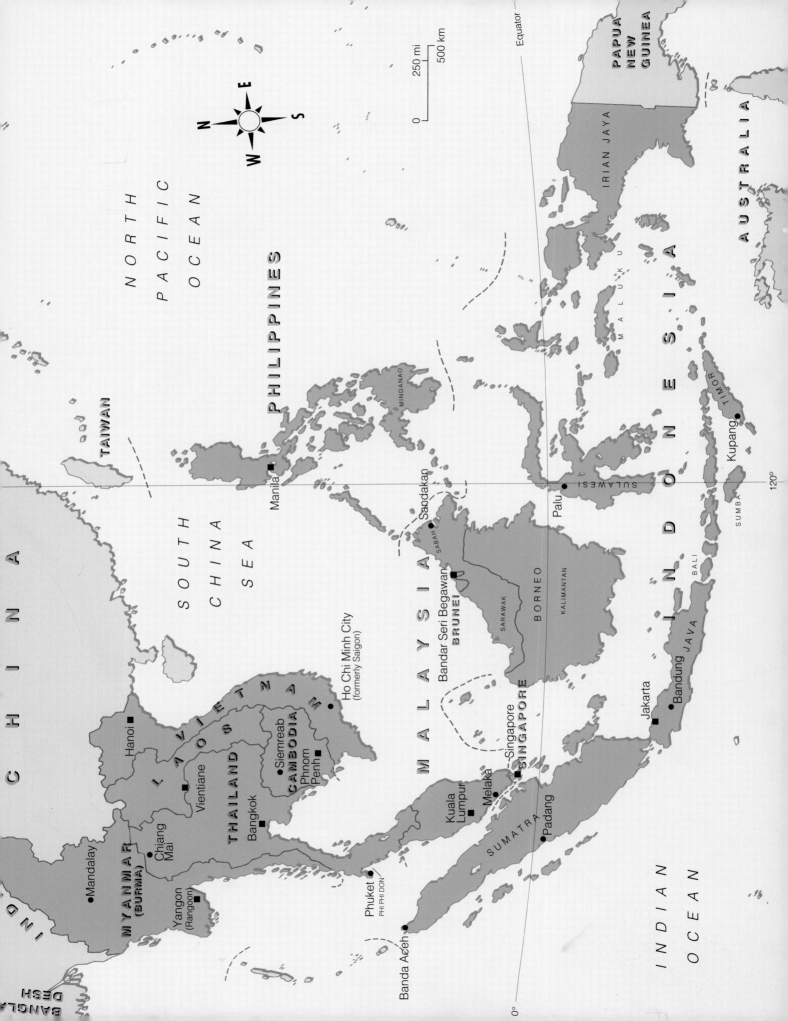

Brunei

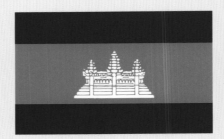

Cambodia

Indonesia

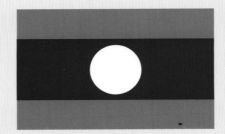

Laos

Malaysia

Myanmar

Philippines

Singapore

Thailand

Vietnam

Southeast Asia

Jonathan Rigg

RAINTREE STECK-VAUGHN
P U B L I S H E R S

Austin, Texas

Published by Raintree Steck-Vaughn Publishers, an imprint of
Steck-Vaughn Company

Design Roger Kohn
Editor Diana Russell, Helene Resky
DTP editor Helen Swansbourne
Picture research Valerie Mulcahy
Illustration János Márffy
Consultant Dr. Michael Parnwell
Commissioning editor Debbie Fox

We are grateful to the following for permission
to reproduce photographs:
Front Cover: TRIP (Linda Jackson) *above*, Tony Stone Images
(Paul Chesley) *below*; Cephas, page 42 (N. J. Bellgrove);
Robert Harding Picture Library, pages 9 *below*, 12 *below*,
16 *above*, 17, 18, 23 (Michael Jenner), 26 *above*, 26 *below*,
36–37 (Photobank), 40 (F. Jack Jackson); The Hutchison
Library, pages 28–29 (Michael MacIntyre), 34 *right*
(R. Ian Lloyd), 35 (Nancy Durrell-McKenna); Magnum, page 36
(Philip J. Griffiths); Christine Osborne/Middle East Pictures,
pages 19, 24, 25 *right*, 34 *left*; Panos Pictures, pages 13
(D. K. Hulcher), 14 (Jeremy Hartley), 20 and 32 *below*
(Chris Stowers), 27 (Ron Giling), 30, 31 (Sean Sprague),
38 and 41 (Jim Holmes); Rex Features, page 11;
Rex Features/Sipa-Press, page 28; Jonathan Rigg, pages
9 *above*, 15, 33; Frank Spooner Pictures/Gamma Press, pages
21 *right*, 44 (Lovigny), 45 (Brown/LSN); Tony Stone Images,
pages 8 (Bob Krist), 10–11 (Paul Berger), 16 *below* (Nigel
Dickinson), 22, 39; TRIP, pages 12 *above* (Terry Knight),
21 *left* (A. R. Barrow), 25 *left*; TRIP/Eye Ubiquitous, page 32
above (Gavin Wickham)

The statistics given in this book are the most up-to-date
available at the time of going to press

Printed and bound in Hong Kong by Paramount Printing Group

2 3 4 5 6 7 8 9 0 HK 99 98 97 96

Library of Congress Cataloging-in-Publication Data
Rigg, Jonathan, 1959–.
Southeast Asia / Jonathan Rigg.
p. cm. — (Country fact files)
Includes index.
ISBN 0-8114-2788-9
1. Asia, Southeastern — Juvenile literature.
I. Title. II. Series.
DS521.R54 1995
959—dc20
94-20444
CIP AC

C O N T E N T S

Words that are explained in the glossary are printed in
SMALL CAPITALS the first time they are mentioned in the text.

Southeast Asia includes ten independent nations with a total population of 452 million and a land area of 1,572,243 square miles (4,071,538 sq km), almost half the size of the United States. They range from the poor COMMUNIST countries of Vietnam and Laos, the rapidly developing democracies of Malaysia and Singapore, the rich monarchy of Brunei, and the military government of Myanmar. There are six major religions and perhaps 1,000 languages in the region.

Europeans arrived in Southeast Asia in the 16th century, when the Portuguese took control of the Indian Ocean and obtained Macao as a port for trade. They were attracted by the riches of the Spice Islands (Maluku) of eastern Indonesia, the only place in the world where nutmeg and cloves were grown. After the Portuguese came the Spanish, Dutch, British, French and Americans, who divided the region among them and exploited its mineral and agricultural resources. Only Thailand kept its independence from outside powers.

Today, Southeast Asia has some of the fastest growing economies in the world. Singapore is a sophisticated international financial center, and Malaysia and Thailand are booming. But there are also areas where life has changed little. The gleaming skyscrapers of cities such as Manila and Bangkok provide a sharp contrast with the poor communities that lie in their shadows. And while the region has modern factories where computers are made, many of its farmers still perform many tasks by hand.

◀ *Singapore's modern high-rise business district towers over a remnant of the original Chinatown, whose old shops are now tourist attractions.*

▶ *In Hanoi, bicycles are the main form of transportation, and old European buildings dominate the city. Political isolation and lack of money mean many cities in north Vietnam have changed little since the 1930s.*

● Population density: 266 people per square mile (103 per sq km)
● Major cities: Jakarta 10 million; Manila 9.6 million; Bangkok 5.8 million; Yangon (Rangoon) 4 million
● Highest mountain: Hkakabo Razi (Myanmar) 19,296 feet (5,881 m)
● Longest river: Mekong, 2,790 miles (4,500 km)
● Major languages: Bahasa Indonesian, Bahasa Malaysian, Thai, Burmese, Vietnamese, Tagalog (Philippines), Lao, Khmer (Cambodia), various Chinese dialects, English
● Major religions: Islam, THERAVADA BUDDHISM, Christianity, MAHAYANA BUDDHISM, CONFUCIANISM, DAOISM
● Major exports: Agricultural commodities (especially rice, rubber, palm oil), timber, fish, shellfish, textiles, electronics, minerals (especially oil, gas, and copper), gemstones

▲ *A poor rice farmer crouches outside his house in northeast Thailand. He only grows enough rice to feed his family, leaving nothing to sell.*

THE LANDSCAPE

Southeast Asia stretches more than 3,720 miles (6,000 km) from the northern hills of Myanmar to the forests of Irian Jaya in Indonesia, which is only 155 miles (250 km) from Australia. There is a broad division between "mainland" and "island" Southeast Asia. Cambodia, Laos, Myanmar, Thailand, and Vietnam make up mainland Southeast Asia. To the north,

Hkakabo Razi
19,296 ft. (5881 m)

MYANMAR

Irrawaddy

Hwang Ho

LAOS

Chao Phraya

THAILAND

VIETNAM

Mekong River

CAMBODIA

SOUTH CHINA SEA

Mount Pinatubo

PHILIPPINES

PACIFIC OCEAN

N

MALAYSIA

Mount Kinabalu
13,451 ft. (4,101 m)

BRUNEI

CELEBES SEA

Lake Toba

0   250 mi
     500 km

SINGAPORE

Mount Jaya
16,500 ft. (5,030 m)

BANDA SEA

Krakatau
2,667 ft. (813 m)

INDONESIA

INDIAN OCEAN

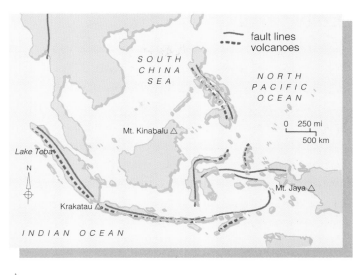

▲ **Like California, Southeast Asia lies over a fault in the earth's crust. Earthquakes and volcanic eruptions can occur.**

▲ *Despite its lush tropical vegetation, Phi Phi Don, off Thailand, has a long dry season.*

▶ *One of the region's highest peaks is Mount Kinabalu in Sabah, Malaysia, 13,451 feet (4,101 m).*

these countries are bounded by a series of mountain chains. The shallow South China Sea separates the mainland from island Southeast Asia, which consists of Brunei, Indonesia, Malaysia, the Philippines, and Singapore. Together, Indonesia and the Philippines are made up of more than 20,000 islands.

Geologically, the region is divided by a series of FAULT LINES, which can produce great, and often violent, volcanic activity, sometimes called a "ring of fire." Indonesia alone has more than 100 active volcanoes. In 1883, the volcano on the island of Krakatau off Java exploded, leaving 36,000 people dead. There are active volcanoes in the Philippines, too. In June 1991, the eruption of Mount Pinatubo left a 6.5-foot- (2-m-) thick blanket of ash over an area stretching 12.5 miles (20 km) from the crater. But after this volcanic ash has broken down, or weathered, it can form highly fertile soils, such as those found on Java.

Southeast Asia is a land of broad valleys, forested uplands, extensive swamps, and dry grasslands. Each environment has been used by people in different ways. The rich river valleys of the Chao Phraya in Thailand, the Mekong and Hwang Ho in Vietnam, and the Irrawaddy in Myanmar have been transformed over the centuries into large areas of rice cultivation. The uplands have either been left as forest and cultivated in small areas or logged and used to plant crops, such as rubber, palm oil, and coffee. In some areas, people have also terraced the hillsides, or leveled sections of it, creating flat land for rice fields. The forests are some of the richest ECOSYSTEMS in the world, with thousands of different tree species and tens of thousands of different flowering plant and insect species.

Higher up into the mountains, the

▲ *In areas such as Timor in eastern Indonesia, little of the ancient forest remains. It is more common now to see areas of open woodland, or savanna.*

▼ *Borneo's dense forests are part of one of the most diverse ecosystems in the world. Rivers are often the only way to reach interior settlements.*

KEY FACTS

● Indonesia consists of 13,677 islands. The Philippines consists of 7,100 islands. Many are no more than coral outcrops.
● The eruption of Krakatau in 1883 was the largest volcanic explosion ever recorded. Its force was 2,000 times greater than the atomic bomb dropped on Hiroshima in 1945.
● The region's largest lake is Lake Toba in Indonesia, 666 square miles (1,707 sq km) in area and 1,738 ft (530 m) deep.

vegetation changes. Above the 4,264-feet- (1,300-m-) line, tropical forest is replaced by temperate trees, such as oak and chestnut. At 6,560 feet (2,000 m) these give way to "cloud" forests with many orchids, rhododendrons, and stunted trees. Higher still, above 9,840 feet (3,000 m), only alpine meadow flowers and mosses can survive the cold. The only glaciers in Southeast Asia are found in the very highest mountains, in Irian Jaya, Indonesia.

The drier islands of Sumba and Timor in Indonesia are more suited to cattle grazing and growing crops like corn and cassava (a root crop). Many of the region's swamps in

places such as Sumatra and Kalimantan, Indonesia, have been left untouched, although the increasing population is forcing people to settle even here to grow swamp rice, often with government aid.

The ocean is also an important feature of Southeast Asia. The region has a longer coastline than any other area of similar size. Laos is the only Southeast Asian country that does not have a coastline, but elsewhere many people live within easy access to the ocean, and fishing is a way of life for large numbers of households. Away from the ocean, rivers and lakes provide people with freshwater fish and crabs.

▼ *Along the Mekong River in south Vietnam, the flat landscape is marked by patchworks of rice fields and scattered settlements.*

CLIMATE AND WEATHER

All the countries of Southeast Asia lie between the Tropics of Cancer and Capricorn. At sea level, temperatures are fairly similar across the region and throughout the year, averaging 79°F (26°C). It is only at high altitudes that temperatures drop significantly. Frosts can occur in highland areas, and people wear sweaters during the chilly nights and early mornings.

But rainfall can vary enormously between different places, and there are also important local differences in climate. In Indonesia, annual rainfall averages only 21 inches (530 mm) in Palu, Sulawesi, while in Padang, Sumatra, it can be ten times greater. The seasonal timing of rainfall is also important. This is determined by the monsoons, or seasonal shifts in

▶**Floods occur yearly in some areas. In Jakarta, local residents continue with their daily chores despite flooded roads and houses.**

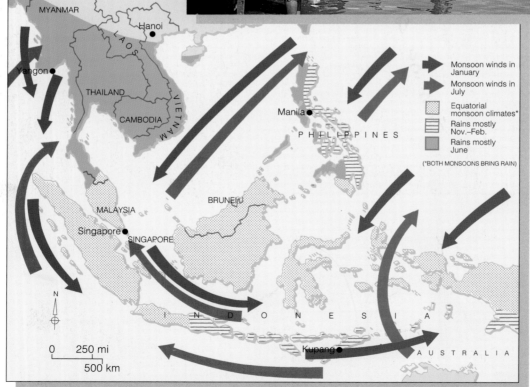

MYANMAR
Hanoi
LAOS
Yangon
THAILAND
VIETNAM
CAMBODIA
Manila
PHILIPPINES

Monsoon winds in January
Monsoon winds in July
Equatorial monsoon climates*
Rains mostly Nov.–Feb.
Rains mostly June
(*BOTH MONSOONS BRING RAIN)

BRUNEI
MALAYSIA
Singapore
SINGAPORE
I N D O N E S I A
N
0   250 mi
500 km
Kupang
A U S T R A L I A

◀**The monsoons bring either wet or dry weather to Southeast Asia.**

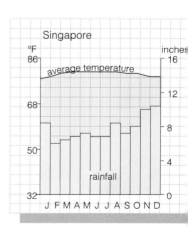

Singapore
°F
86
average temperature
68
50
32
rainfall
J F M A M J J A S O N D

inches
16
12
8
4
0

wind, which bring either rain or dry conditions. Unlike temperate countries such as the United States, in Southeast Asia it is rainfall, not temperature, that divides the seasons. Some farmers still perform special "rain-making" rituals if the rains are late.

The region can be divided into three climate zones. To the north, rain tends to fall between June and September. Near the equator, it can fall at any time. To the south and east, it is concentrated between November and February. The dry season also tends to last longer farther away from the equator. So Singapore, which is almost on the equator, has no dry season. But Chiang Mai in Thailand to the north and Kupang in Indonesia to the south both have dry seasons six months long. Kupang's dry season runs from April to September and Chiang Mai's from November to April.

Extremes of climate can be terribly destructive. In the Philippines, TYPHOONS with wind speeds of more than 62 miles per hour (100 kph) can destroy houses, devastate crops, and kill hundreds of people. In every country, rains bring not only the hope of good crops, but also the threat of floods. In 1988, landslides following heavy rains in south Thailand killed 300 villagers.

▲ *During the dry season in Thailand, fields become very parched.*

KEY FACTS

● The word *monsoon* comes from Arabic *mawsim*, meaning "season."
● The highlands of Irian Jaya, Indonesia, are one of the wettest places on Earth. Rainfall averages 320 inches (8,000 mm) per year.
● Over much of Thailand, Myanmar, and Laos, 80–90 percent of the rain falls between May and October.

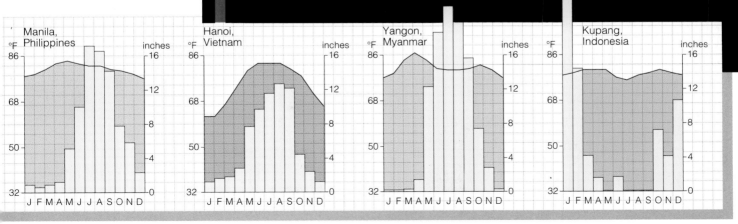

NATURAL RESOURCES

◀ *An oil rig in a forest in Sumatra, Indonesia. Some oil companies fly all workers and materials in by helicopter. Because roads are not needed, there is less disruption to wildlife.*

▼ *Timber is one of Malaysia's most important exports. Here, a man with a chainsaw fells a tropical hardwood tree.*

During the 19th century, natural resources, such as tin, teak, and spices, made Southeast Asia attractive to the COLONIAL powers. By 1930, Malaysia, Thailand, and Indonesia produced 60 percent of the world's trade in tin. Today, the figure is still more than 50 percent. Oil and natural gas have also become important. Indonesia, Malaysia, and Brunei are major exporters. Other minerals include coal,

KEY FACTS

● The Freeport Indonesia mine in Irian Jaya has the biggest gold reserves of any mine in the world (worth $15 billion).
● Malaysia is the world's second largest exporter of rough timber (the United States is the largest).
● Laos earns $15 million a year by exporting hydroelectric power.

▶ *Tin mining was once Malaysia's chief industry. Many mines have closed down, but in parts of west Malaysia the industry still generates wealth and employment.*

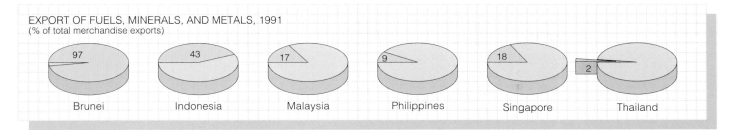

EXPORT OF FUELS, MINERALS, AND METALS, 1991
(% of total merchandise exports)

Brunei	Indonesia	Malaysia	Philippines	Singapore	Thailand
97	43	17	9	18	2

gold, copper, and gemstones, particularly rubies and sapphires from Myanmar, Cambodia, and Thailand.

Plantation crops, such as rubber, coffee, and tea, were grown widely in colonial times, when large estates were set up. Some big estates remain, but smaller plantations owned by individual families are important, too. Malaysia, Indonesia, and Thailand now produce 82 percent of the world's trade in rubber.

Malaysia, Indonesia, and other countries export tropical timber, mostly to Japan, where it is used in construction or made into disposable chopsticks. The loss of the region's forests has been so rapid that Thailand, once a major exporter, now imports wood. Wood is also an important source of energy. Most rural families cook using charcoal and wood fires.

The rivers of Southeast Asia have been used to generate hydroelectric power. Like logging, constructing dams has become controversial because of their impact on local people and on the environment.

POPULATION

POPULATION DISTRIBUTION

The distribution of Southeast Asia's 452 million inhabitants is very uneven. Indonesia has the world's fourth largest population (after China, India, and the United States), with more than 187 million people, while Brunei has only 300,000 inhabitants. About 60 percent of Indonesia's population — more than 100 million people — live on Java, an island that covers only 6 percent of the country's land area. Irian Jaya, over three times the size of Java, has fewer than 2 million inhabitants. This uneven distribution has led governments to resettle people in new villages in remote areas. In Indonesia, more than 6 million have been resettled since 1950.

Although there are still areas where few people live, since the 1970s, most of the countries in the region have introduced policies of family planning to limit population growth. Only in Malaysia is the government trying to increase the size of families.

MIGRATION AND CITY GROWTH

Most of Southeast Asia's inhabitants live in rural areas where life seems to have changed little. But modernization has encouraged the movement of people from the countryside to towns and cities. Some work in urban areas for only part of the year before returning to their villages, a process known as circulation. Many others settle permanently in towns and cities.

Migration explains why the urban population of Southeast Asia is growing twice as fast as the average elsewhere in

POPULATION

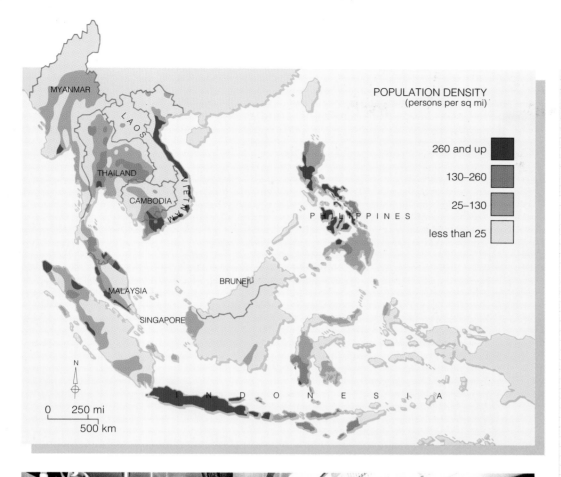

POPULATION DENSITY
(persons per sq mi)

- 260 and up
- 130–260
- 25–130
- less than 25

0 250 mi
500 km

N

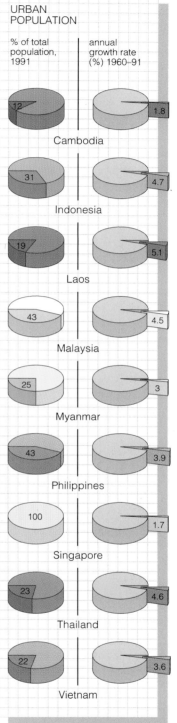

URBAN POPULATION

% of total population, 1991 | annual growth rate (%) 1960–91

Cambodia 12 | 1.8
Indonesia 31 | 4.7
Laos 19 | 5.1
Malaysia 43 | 4.5
Myanmar 25 | 3
Philippines 43 | 3.9
Singapore 100 | 1.7
Thailand 23 | 4.6
Vietnam 22 | 3.6

◄ **Women cook food over open palmwood fires in a Cambodian village near Siemreab. Malnutrition is common in rural areas.**

▲ **Improved transportation and better job prospects have encouraged people to move to urban areas.**

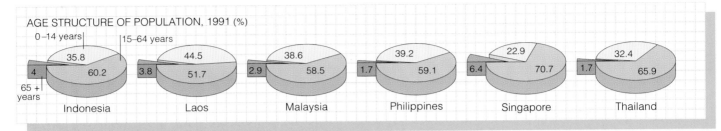

AGE STRUCTURE OF POPULATION, 1991 (%)

0–14 years | 15–64 years | 65 + years

	0–14	15–64	65+
Indonesia	35.8	60.2	4
Laos	44.5	51.7	3.8
Malaysia	38.6	58.5	2.9
Philippines	39.2	59.1	1.7
Singapore	22.9	70.7	6.4
Thailand	32.4	65.9	1.7

▲ **The tribal peoples of Borneo are known as Dayaks. The island has about 200 tribes with different customs, languages, and life-styles.**

the world. It also means that official statistics for the population of cities are often too low. For instance, the population of Bangkok is officially less than 6 million, but most experts believe it is closer to 11 million. The movement of people to urban areas has stimulated the growth of slums. It has also made problems such as traffic congestion and pollution more severe.

ETHNIC MINORITIES

Southeast Asia's ethnic minorities include several groups of tribal peoples, who live in the mountains of Thailand, Myanmar, Laos, and Vietnam, such as the Hmong and Paduang, and in the forests of Malaysia, the Philippines, and Indonesia, such as the Iban

POPULATION DENSITY PER SQUARE MILE, 1991

131.8	Brunei	48.7 Laos
125.6	Cambodia	145.3 Malaysia
268.3	Indonesia	168.4 Myanmar
		554.4 Philippines
11,574		Singapore
		280.8 Thailand
	542	Vietnam

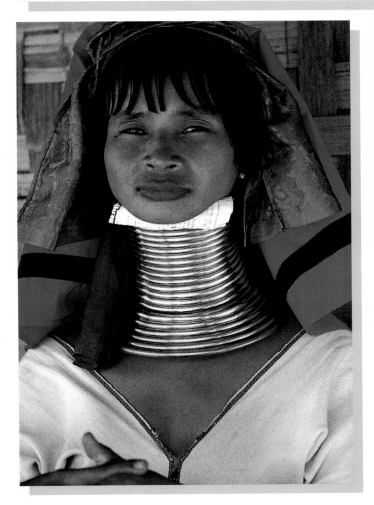

▲ *Since 1976 more than a million boat people have fled Vietnam because of persecution and poverty. Here, a group awaits rescue from their overloaded boat. Today, the flood of refugees has almost stopped.*

◄ *The "Long-Neck Karen," or Padaung, live in the hills of Laos, northern Thailand, and Myanmar. From childhood, female Padaung slowly add rings around their necks to lengthen them. Their necks can reach 12 inches (30 cm).*

and Dani. They are often poor and rarely have political or economic influence.

Another ethnic group, the Chinese, have become very prosperous, although there are poor Chinese, too. Most have emigrated from China since the late 19th century, coming to Southeast Asia to work in tin mines as laborers, or to run small businesses. Today, many of the largest companies in the area are owned by people of Chinese origin.

KEY FACTS

● Southeast Asia has nearly 25 million ethnic Chinese inhabitants.
● Five hundred eighty-three dialects or languages are spoken in Indonesia alone.
● Bangkok's population of 5.8 million is more than 20 times larger than that of Thailand's second largest city, Chiang Mai.
● Indians make up 9 percent of Malaysia's population.

For rich and poor, farmers and factory workers, Muslims and Buddhists, men and women, young and old, daily life varies. However, the family plays an important role in life throughout the region. Unlike the West, where the rights of the individual tend to be stressed, in Southeast Asia the individual often bows to the needs of the family. For example, daughters from rural families who go to work in cities such as Manila or Bangkok, usually send money home to help support their brothers and sisters. Although marriages are rarely arranged by families, few young people marry without their parents' consent. Newly married couples tend to live with their parents or parents-in-law. But these traditions are changing. In Singapore and other modern cities, some young people are choosing to live apart from their families. They find extended family life too restricting.

EDUCATION

Before the 20th century, the only schools open to most people were those attached to religious centers. Young men were taught to read and write in Buddhist monasteries and Muslim mosques. For most girls, education was not available. As the countries of Southeast Asia have grown richer and factories more advanced, the value of a good education has grown in importance. Primary school enrollment (which is compulsory and free in most cases) and literacy rates are high. But at secondary school level and above, enrollment rates are much lower. Very few young people seek higher education, and even fewer enroll in engineering and science courses. An exception is the Philippines, where 27 percent of the students go to

▼ *A family in Sarawak, Malaysia, eats a meal sitting on mats. Family members help themselves from dishes placed in the center. Food is often eaten with the fingers.*

THE OFFICIAL LANGUAGES
OF SOUTHEAST ASIA

BRUNEI:
English, Malay

CAMBODIA:
Khmer

INDONESIA:
Bahasa Indonesian

LAOS:
Lao

MALAYSIA:
Bahasa Malaysian

MYANMAR:
Burmese

PHILIPPINES:
English, Filipino, or Tagalog

SINGAPORE:
Bahasa Malaysian, Mandarin
Chinese, English, Tamil

THAILAND:
Thai

VIETNAM:
Vietnamese

KEY FACTS

● On average, students in the Philippines spend more than 7 years in school.

● Myanmar, Laos, and Cambodia are three of the world's poorest countries, with an average annual income of only $180 per person. Brunei is one of the richest, with an income of $15,200 per person.

● In Thailand there are 30,000 Buddhist monasteries and 340,000 monks and novices (monks in training).

● In Myanmar, 175,000 children under the age of 5 die each year, and 80 percent of primary schoolchildren fail to complete 5 years of education.

● In Brunei, people pay no income tax. They receive free education, medical care, and retirement pensions.

● The Temple of Literature in Hanoi was Vietnam's first "university." It was founded in A.D. 1070.

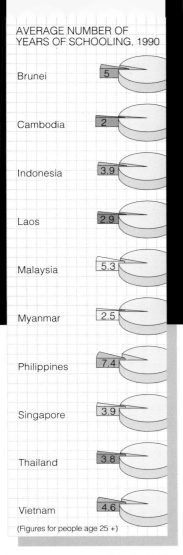

AVERAGE NUMBER OF YEARS OF SCHOOLING, 1990

Country	Years
Brunei	5
Cambodia	2
Indonesia	3.9
Laos	2.9
Malaysia	5.3
Myanmar	2.5
Philippines	7.4
Singapore	3.9
Thailand	3.8
Vietnam	4.6

(Figures for people age 25 +)

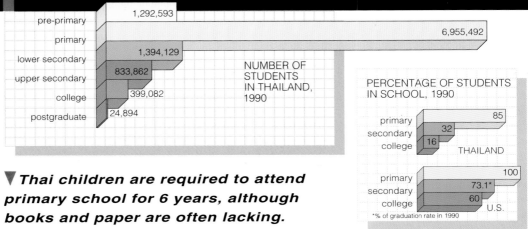

NUMBER OF STUDENTS IN THAILAND, 1990

Level	Students
pre-primary	1,292,593
primary	6,955,492
lower secondary	1,394,129
upper secondary	833,862
college	399,082
postgraduate	24,894

PERCENTAGE OF STUDENTS IN SCHOOL, 1990

THAILAND

Level	%
primary	85
secondary	32
college	16

U.S.

Level	%
primary	100
secondary	73.1*
college	60

*% of graduation rate in 1990

▼ **Thai children are required to attend primary school for 6 years, although books and paper are often lacking.**

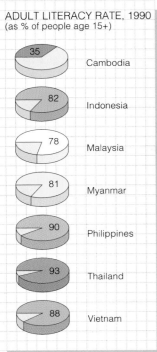

ADULT LITERACY RATE, 1990
(as % of people age 15+)

Cambodia	35
Indonesia	82
Malaysia	78
Myanmar	81
Philippines	90
Thailand	93
Vietnam	88

college or a university. (More than 60 percent of high school graduates in the United States receive some type of advanced schooling.) Elsewhere, the low level of education is worrying many people, because they see it limiting economic development. Thailand, for instance, already has a severe shortage of engineers, forcing some companies to employ people from overseas.

RELIGION

Political leaders in Southeast Asia sometimes worry that people are losing their religious beliefs as they increasingly come into contact with Western ideas. But religion is still one of the keystones of daily life in the region. The *wat,* or monastery, in Thailand and Laos, the pagoda, or temple, in Vietnam, the church in the Philippines, and the mosque in Indonesia and Malaysia are focal points of

local life. Monks, priests, and imams are highly respected. They are called on for advice and help to settle local disputes. So too are shamans, or witch doctors, among those few people who are still ANIMISTS.

LEISURE

In the past, entertainment was often linked

DISTRIBUTION OF RELIGIONS

MYANMAR

LAOS

THAILAND

CAMBODIA

VIETNAM

SOUTH
CHINA
SEA

PHILIPPINES

BRUNEI

MALAYSIA

SINGAPORE

INDONESIA

Animist
(undergoing conversion)

Christian

Hindu

Muslim

Theravada Buddhist

Mahayana Buddhist,
Confucianist, and Daoist

▲*People in Bali, Indonesia, are mainly Hindu. Here, girls in traditional clothes pray during a ceremony in a Hindu temple, or* pura.

with traditional religious festivals, such as the water festival in Thailand, Laos, and Myanmar, which is celebrated to mark the end of the dry season. Seasonal foods were cooked, and traveling theater groups and musicians provided entertainment. People would also play traditional games such as kite fighting and spinning tops, while

RELIGIOUS FESTIVALS OF SOUTHEAST ASIA

Most of Southeast Asia's religious festivals are based on the lunar calendar, so, like Easter Sunday, the dates vary from year to year.

BUDDHIST FESTIVALS
(celebrated mainly in Thailand, Myanmar, Laos, and Cambodia)

February
● MAGHA PUJA – celebrates the assembly of the Buddha's disciples to hear him preach. Candlelit processions are held in many monasteries.

April
● SONGKRAN – marks the beginning of the Buddhist New Year, when birds and fish are set free

June
● VISAKHA PUJA – the holiest of all the Buddhist festivals, it marks the birth, enlightenment, and death of the Buddha. Candlelit festivals are held at many monasteries.

August
● ASALHA PUJA and KHAO PHANSA – marks the occasion of the Buddha's first sermon and the beginning of the Buddhist Lent. Monks stay in their monasteries to meditate.

October
● OK PHANSA – marks the end of the Buddhist Lent and the beginning of Kathin, when gifts are offered to the monks

MUSLIM FESTIVALS
(celebrated mainly in Indonesia, Malaysia, and Brunei)

March/April
● HARI RAYA PUASA or IDUL FITRI – a 2-day festival marking the end of the month-long period of Ramadan when Muslims fast from dawn to dusk

July
● HARI RAYA HAJI – marks the return of pilgrims from Mecca

July/August
● MAAL HIJRAH – marks the beginning of the Muslim calendar when the Prophet Muhammad journeyed from Mecca to Medina

August/September
● GAREBAG MAULAD or MAULUD NABI – marks the birthday of the Prophet Muhammad

CHINESE FESTIVALS
(celebrated mainly in Vietnam, Singapore, and Malaysia)

February
● CHINESE NEW YEAR – the lunar New Year, celebrated over 15 days with great enthusiasm; in Vietnam known as "Tet"

August
● WANDERING SOULS DAY or the FESTIVAL OF THE HUNGRY GHOSTS – prayers are said to cancel out the sins of the dead; food is placed on tables, and money is burned.

August/September
● MOON CAKE or MID-AUTUMN FESTIVAL – celebrates the overthrow of the Mongol Dynasty in China, when people exchange moon cakes. It is also a harvest festival.

CHRISTIAN FESTIVALS
(celebrated mainly in the Philippines, Singapore, Vietnam, and Indonesia)

March/April
● EASTER

December
● CHRISTMAS – celebrated across the region, but religious aspects are often ignored except by Christians

HINDU FESTIVALS
(celebrated mainly in Malaysia)

January
● THAIPUSAM – Hindu festival in honor of the deity Lord Subramanian, when participants pierce their bodies with skewers and hooks

November
● DEEPVALI – the Hindu festival of lights, marking the victory of light over darkness

▲ *The Omar Ali Saifuddin Mosque in Bandar Seri Begawan, built in 1958, is the religious focus for Brunei's Muslims.*

▶ *Chinese religions include ancestor worship. This is a Daoist ancestor shrine in Cheng Hoon Teng Temple in Melaka, Malaysia.*

▶ **April is the month of the water festival, called "Thingyan," in Mandalay, Myanmar. It marks the end of the dry season and is celebrated with much water-throwing.**

▼ **These billboards in Bangkok advertise Thai and Chinese films. American films dubbed into Thai are also very popular.**

▶ **Smoky Mountain is a massive garbage dump outside of Manila. Here, poor families, including young children, hunt for anything of value they can find. Tin cans and plastic are sold for recycling, bringing a meager income. The families live in the dump, and are exposed to the unhygienic conditions that surround them.**

masked dances, like the *lakhon* in Thailand, and puppet shows, like the *wayang* in Malaysia and Indonesia, were performed. Such shows were accompanied by music played on traditional instruments.

Traditional forms of sports and entertainment are still very popular. But today, the radio, television, movies, discos, and karaoke bars provide new types of entertainment, mostly in towns and especially for the young.

SOCIAL TENSIONS

The people of Southeast Asia also have many problems. Some of these are old problems that have yet to be resolved, but others are new ones, often linked to modernization. The position of women in society remains unequal. Very few women achieve high positions in politics or business, few have secondary or higher education, and in family life men are dominant. Poverty is also a continuing problem. Despite rapid economic growth, in some rural areas more than 50 percent of families are defined as poor. This brings other problems: bad nutrition, high rates of infant mortality, and inadequate sanitation. In Laos, for example, 37 percent of the children under age five are malnourished, more than one in ten infants die, and only 11 percent of the population has access to sanitation.

There are also some new problems. Drug abuse and crime are increasing. And wars in Myanmar, Laos, and Cambodia have led to the migration of hundreds of thousands of refugees to neighboring countries.

RULES AND LAWS

Those countries of Southeast Asia that were ruled by outside powers achieved independence after World War II, most between 1946 and 1963. Since then, only Singapore and Malaysia have experienced democratic rule without interruption.

One major division that appeared was between the Communist countries of Vietnam, Laos, and Cambodia and the rest

▼ *Thailand's King Bhumibol is greatly respected by his people. He tours the countryside, visiting villages and supporting development projects.*

▶ *In February 1986 "people power" in the Philippines forced President Marcos to flee to the United States. He is said to have stolen $5 billion of public money. Here, supporters of Corazón Aquino, who succeeded him, celebrate their victory.*

KEY FACTS

● More bombs were dropped during the Vietnam War than during all previous wars combined.
● Sultan Hassanal Bolkiah of Brunei is reputed to be the world's richest man, with a fortune of $37 billion.
● The military have either taken over the government in Thailand, or tried to do so, 17 times since 1945.
● Until 1989 Myanmar was known as Burma, and the capital Yangon as Rangoon.

SYSTEMS OF GOVERNMENT

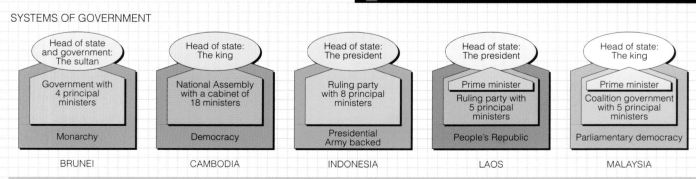

Head of state and government: The sultan	Head of state: The king	Head of state: The president	Head of state: The president	Head of state: The king
Government with 4 principal ministers	National Assembly with a cabinet of 18 ministers	Ruling party with 8 principal ministers	Prime minister / Ruling party with 5 principal ministers	Prime minister / Coalition government with 5 principal ministers
Monarchy	Democracy	Presidential Army backed	People's Republic	Parliamentary democracy
BRUNEI	CAMBODIA	INDONESIA	LAOS	MALAYSIA

Suharto, have ruled since 1945. And in the Philippines, Ferdinand Marcos was president from 1965 to 1986. These leaders have provided stability, but sometimes they have persecuted groups of their people and ignored human rights. Corruption has also been a problem. Only recently has the demand for more democratic and professional government grown stronger.

Kings or sultans reign in four countries. Brunei is the only absolute monarchy, which means the sultan rules by himself, with no government. In Malaysia, the nine hereditary sultans take turns as king for five years each, but political power lies with the democratically elected prime minister. The monarchy in Cambodia was restored in 1993. In Thailand, King Bhumibol is a constitutional monarch, like Queen Elizabeth II of the United Kingdom. But he has great influence and has sometimes forced corrupt governments to resign.

The armed forces are highly influential in politics throughout Southeast Asia. In Indonesia, the army leads the ruling party, Sekber Golkar (Joint Secretariat of Functional Groups). Armed forces in the region often see themselves as the protectors of the people in the face of corrupt and selfish politicians.

of the region. It was concern over the spread of Communism that led the United States into the Vietnam War between 1964 and 1973. Communist governments remain in control in Vietnam and Laos today, but relations between them and their neighbors are much improved.

Strong leaders have been a feature of Southeast Asia. In Myanmar, General Ne Win was in control from 1962 until 1988. In Singapore, Lee Kuan Yew was prime minister for 31 years until 1990. In Indonesia, just two presidents, Sukarno and

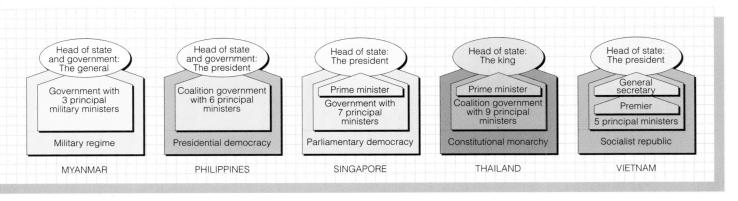

Head of state and government: The general	Head of state and government: The president	Head of state: The president	Head of state: The king	Head of state: The president
Government with 3 principal military ministers	Coalition government with 6 principal ministers	Prime minister	Prime minister	General secretary
		Government with 7 principal ministers	Coalition government with 9 principal ministers	Premier
				5 principal ministers
Military regime	Presidential democracy	Parliamentary democracy	Constitutional monarchy	Socialist republic
MYANMAR	PHILIPPINES	SINGAPORE	THAILAND	VIETNAM

FOOD AND FARMING

Southeast Asia is still predominantly a region of farmers. Although industrial growth is rapid, more than half the population live on the land. Most work and own small family farms. In Java, Indonesia, farms average about one acre (0.5 ha). There are relatively few large landowners.

Rice is Southeast Asia's most important crop. It is first sown in nursery beds and then transplanted into fields where it grows standing in water. Yields can be more than 5 tons per 2.5 acres (one ha). Where the land is IRRIGATED, two or three crops are grown each year in each field. Some rice-growing areas of Java support 2,000 people in half a square mile (about one sq km). Thailand and Vietnam are two of the world's largest exporters of the crop.

Rice is also grown in dry conditions, often by tribal people. This is known as slash-and-burn agriculture. These farmers clear the forest, burn the trees, and plant crops such as rice, corn, and cassava in the ash. After a few years, the field is abandoned because the land becomes less fertile, and another plot is cleared. With growing populations and concern for the environment, this type of agriculture is now becoming less common. In some upland areas, it is being replaced by plantation crops. These are often tree crops, like rubber and palm oil, which help protect

the land by binding the soil and preventing it from being washed away by heavy rain. Many plantation crops need to be processed before they can be sold. Large plantations have their own processing plants, but small landowners depend on plants built by the government.

Around cities and towns, farmers grow vegetables and fruit to feed the urban population. Farms can be very small, but they are highly productive. Fish are also an important part of the diet of Southeast Asians, and they are sold live in many markets. Freshwater fish are raised in ponds. Saltwater fish are transported from the coast, where trawlers and small fishing boats work the rich oceans.

In drier parts of Southeast Asia, such as eastern Indonesia and northeast Thailand, cattle ranching is important. Overgrazing in some areas, like Timor, Indonesia, has led to

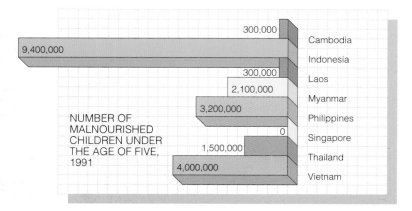

NUMBER OF MALNOURISHED CHILDREN UNDER THE AGE OF FIVE, 1991

Cambodia	300,000
Indonesia	9,400,000
Laos	300,000
Myanmar	2,100,000
Philippines	3,200,000
Singapore	0
Thailand	1,500,000
Vietnam	4,000,000

◀ *Large-scale commercial plantations are common in Southeast Asia. Here, workers harvest pineapples in Mindanao, south Philippines. The fruit is canned and exported.*

▼ *Workers transplant rice seedlings into a prepared paddy field in west Java, Indonesia. It is hard work but helps produce high yields on small farms.*

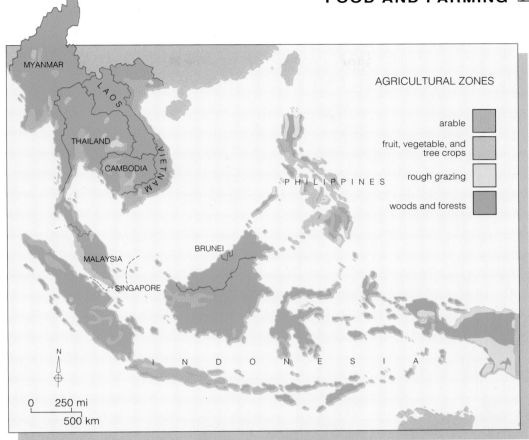

AGRICULTURAL ZONES

arable

fruit, vegetable, and tree crops

rough grazing

woods and forests

MYANMAR

LAOS

THAILAND

CAMBODIA

VIETNAM

PHILIPPINES

MALAYSIA

SINGAPORE

BRUNEI

INDONESIA

N

0   250 mi

500 km

a loss of grassland. New, hardy fodder crops have been introduced to improve the land. Pigs and chickens are important farm animals, too.

Population growth means that some farmers have no land or have farms too small to feed their families. They must either work on other people's land or move to the towns to find a job. Governments have sometimes tried to take land from the rich to give to the poor, a process known as land reform. This was very important in the Communist countries of Vietnam, Laos, and Cambodia. Governments have also tried to increase production through the "Green Revolution." This involves growing new crops, using large quantities of fertilizers and pesticides.

▼ *A Malaysian plantation worker cuts the bark of a rubber tree to start the flow of latex. This is later collected and processed into rubber.*

◀ *Insects and other nutritious "forest products" are still eaten in many countries of Southeast Asia. Here, a girl sells deep-fried locusts at the side of a street in Myanmar.*

▶ *Water buffalo are used to plow rice fields. In Sulawesi they are also sacrificed at funeral ceremonies.*

Yields can be very high, but some people worry about the environmental effects of these poisons.

The diet of most Southeast Asians includes rice, fresh fruits and vegetables, fish, and meat. Strongly spiced foods are popular. LEMONGRASS, hot peppers, coriander, and spicy fish sauces are common. Coconut is often used in cooking, especially to make creamy curries. The large Chinese population ensures that Chinese foods are widely sold. Religion plays a part in people's diets. Muslims will not eat pork or drink alcohol, while many Hindus and Buddhist monks are vegetarians.

Today, tastes in the region are changing. Bread can be bought in many towns, and fast-food restaurants are spreading. Traditional foods, such as insects, are becoming less popular. Once it was common for people to chew betel nuts (the nut of the areca palm, wrapped in the leaf of the betel vine and smeared with lime), but fewer people do so now.

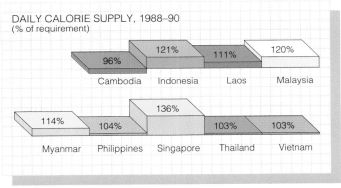

DAILY CALORIE SUPPLY, 1988–90
(% of requirement)

Cambodia	Indonesia	Laos	Malaysia
96%	121%	111%	120%

Myanmar	Philippines	Singapore	Thailand	Vietnam
114%	104%	136%	103%	103%

KEY FACTS

● The rubber tree was introduced from Brazil in the 19th century.
● Thailand is the world's largest exporter of canned tuna.
● The world's first "high-yielding variety" of rice, on which the Green Revolution is based, was bred in the Philippines.
● Vietnam has 20 million bomb craters. Farmers have turned many into fish ponds or use them to irrigate vegetable plots.

TRADE AND INDUSTRY

Southeast Asia includes some of the richest and most advanced countries in Asia, along with some of the poorest in the world. In Singapore, skilled workers produce computers and manage banks. In Myanmar, industry is weak, and exports are limited to products such as timber and fish. All the countries are seeing change as industry becomes more important and agriculture less so.

CAPITALISM AND COMMUNISM

Until recently, the CAPITALIST countries (Brunei, Indonesia, Malaysia, Philippines, Singapore, Thailand) and Communist or Socialist countries (Cambodia, Laos, Myanmar, Vietnam) took different roads to industrialization. The capitalist countries

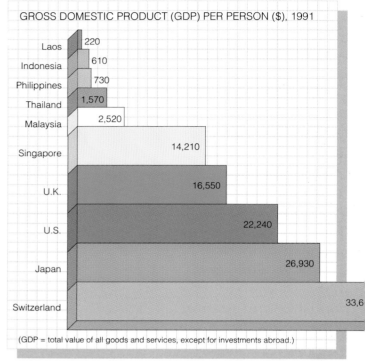

GROSS DOMESTIC PRODUCT (GDP) PER PERSON ($), 1991

Laos	220
Indonesia	610
Philippines	730
Thailand	1,570
Malaysia	2,520
Singapore	14,210
U.K.	16,550
U.S.	22,240
Japan	26,930
Switzerland	33,6

(GDP = total value of all goods and services, except for investments abroad.)

▲ *Malaysia produces the region's only local car — the Proton Saga. It is based on Japanese technology and sells very well, both in Malaysia and in the West.*

◄ *Modern high-technology industries are being set up in Southeast Asia. In Singapore, workers in a dust-free "clean room" check computer disk drives.*

encouraged foreign investment and private businesses. In Indonesia, Malaysia, the Philippines, and Thailand, foreign investment totaled $7.5 billion in 1991. In the Communist countries, the government controlled the economy. Today, Cambodia is no longer a Communist country. The others now welcome foreign investment and are "privatizing" state-owned factories.

TYPES OF PRODUCTION

Small-scale production in the region includes people working at home, making products such as sandals, handicrafts, or cooked foods. Village industries may involve making pottery, mats, and metal tools for local use.

Small firms may make plastic or metal toys using simple technology. Larger factories produce clothing or electronics for export. Some of these factories are owned by foreign companies, which are attracted by the low wages paid in the region. A textile worker in the Philippines or Indonesia is paid an average of $2 a day, in Vietnam even less. Working conditions can be poor, and accidents are common. In May 1993, 200 workers were killed in a fire at a toy factory outside Bangkok because of a lack of fire precautions.

Governments have invested in important projects like the massive Krakatau steelworks

▼ *Handcrafted items, such as woven baskets in the Philippines, provide the chance to work at home in rural areas. This slows the rate of migration to the cities.*

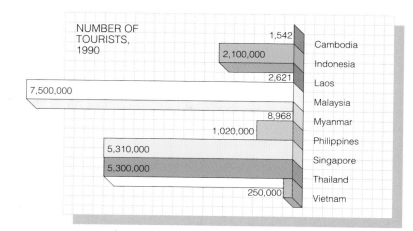

NUMBER OF TOURISTS, 1990

Cambodia	1,542
Indonesia	2,100,000
Laos	2,621
Malaysia	7,500,000
Myanmar	8,968
Philippines	1,020,000
Singapore	5,310,000
Thailand	5,300,000
Vietnam	250,000

▲ *A worker at the state-owned Vietnamese firm Viettronics assembles televisions, using parts made in Japan and South Korea.*

in Java, Indonesia, which cost $4 billion to build and is the largest in Southeast Asia. In the Philippines the government has even built a nuclear power station. High-technology projects include Indonesia's aircraft industry, based near Bandung.

TOURISM, TRADE, AND AID

In 1990, Southeast Asia had more than 20 million tourists, including people within the region vacationing in a neighboring country.

This brought nearly $15 billion into the area. But some local people worry about the effects of tourism on the environment and culture.

Most of Southeast Asia's trade is with the United States, Japan, and Europe. Brunei, Indonesia, Malaysia, the Philippines, Singapore, and Thailand are members of the Association of Southeast Asian Nations (ASEAN), which is trying to encourage more trade within the region.

Thailand, Malaysia, and Singapore also give small amounts of aid to their poorer neighbors, to help them to develop. Only a few years ago, these donor countries were too poor themselves to give help in this way.

KEY FACTS

● Singapore has the highest "trade dependency" of any country in the world. The value of exports and imports is more than three times the country's GDP.
● The Proton Saga accounts for two out of every three cars sold in Malaysia.
● Malaysia is the world's largest producer of semiconductors, which are used in the electronics industry, and air conditioners.
● Oil and gas account for more than 95 percent of Brunei's exports.
● The United States' ban on trade with Vietnam, introduced after the Vietnam War, was not lifted until 1994.
● Laos was severely affected by the Vietnam War. Debris from the war is now one of its most valuable exports.

◄ *Income from tourism is vital for Southeast Asia's economies. Here, some of the 5 million tourists who visit Thailand each year lie on Phuket's Patong Beach.*

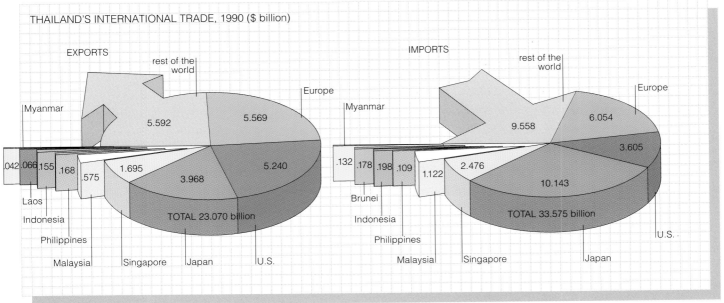

THAILAND'S INTERNATIONAL TRADE, 1990 ($ billion)

EXPORTS — rest of the world, Europe, Myanmar, Laos, Indonesia, Philippines, Malaysia, Singapore, Japan, U.S.
.042, .066, .155, .168, .575, 1.695, 3.968, 5.240, 5.569, 5.592
TOTAL 23.070 billion

IMPORTS — rest of the world, Europe, Myanmar, Brunei, Indonesia, Philippines, Malaysia, Singapore, Japan, U.S.
.132, .178, .198, .109, 1.122, 2.476, 10.143, 9.558, 6.054, 3.605
TOTAL 33.575 billion

A good transportation system is vital to a growing economy. It links markets and people, helps the movement of goods, and makes remote areas accessible. In Vietnam, Laos, and Cambodia, the Vietnam War destroyed bridges and roads. Many still need to be rebuilt. In Myanmar, the government is too poor to invest in roads and railroads. However, elsewhere in the region there has been a transportation revolution. There are passenger railroad networks in all the countries except Brunei and Laos, but inexpensive buses are far more important than trains for carrying both goods and passengers. In Indonesia, for example, a bus from Banda Aceh at the northern tip of Sumatra to the island of Bali costs only $30 for a trip of about 2,480 miles (4,000 km).

Affordable ships and boats link the many islands of Southeast Asia. They travel up rivers, too, carrying passengers and goods. But overcrowding and poor safety standards can cause large-scale disasters. In 1994, 200 people drowned when an overloaded ferry, traveling from Thailand to Myanmar, capsized. Air travel is now growing very rapidly, and international airlines, such as Singapore Airlines and Thai Airways, are among the world's best.

In towns and cities, increased car ownership among the rapidly growing middle class has led to greater traffic congestion. Bangkok probably has the worst traffic of any capital city. Average traffic speeds can be less than 3 miles per hour (5 kph) in the center, and in 1992 one traffic jam took 11 hours to clear. There are also some very distinctive forms of transportation in the region, such as the pedicab, which is inexpensive to use.

NUMBER OF PASSENGER CARS, 1985–89
(per thousand people)

Indonesia	7
Malaysia	91
Myanmar	2
Philippines	6
Singapore	100
Thailand	15

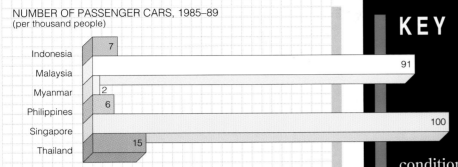

◀ *Pedicabs are an important form of transportation in the region, such as here in Phnom Penh. They offer affordable travel for local people and provide jobs for many poor migrants from the villages.*

▼ *Intercity buses, such as this extravagant one in the Philippines, offer the least expensive form of long-distance travel. Drivers spend weeks decorating them.*

KEY FACTS

● Eight hundred new cars are registered in Bangkok every day.
● Singapore is the only city in Southeast Asia with a subway. It opened in 1987, is fully air-conditioned, and has 42 stations.
● Around Sabah and Sarawak, express riverboats are often the fastest way to travel. They reach speeds of 43 miles per hour (70 kph).
● Indonesia's fleet of sail-powered cargo boats is one of the largest in the world. It has around 1,000 vessels, each weighing between 2 and 200 tons.

THE ENVIRONMENT

The Southeast Asian region contains some of the world's most diverse environments. Nearly 200 species of trees can be found growing in 2.5 acres (1 ha) of tropical forest in Malaysia or Indonesia, and there are more than 25,000 species of flowering plants in the area — about 10 percent of the world's total. Some of the rarest animals are also found in the region, for example, the Javan rhinoceros, of which there are less than 100 alive today. Other animals that have been hunted close to extinction include the orangutan, the kouprey of Cambodia (a type of giant wild cattle), the tiger, and the sea turtle.

The governments of the region have created national parks to protect these animals and plants. Most have been set up since the 1960s. Thailand's first national park, Khao Yai, was established in 1961. Today, the country has 63 parks, covering more than 9,650 square miles (25,000 sq km), 5 percent of its land area. Unfortunately, most countries do not have the money to maintain these parks properly, and logging and poaching are still common. The economies of Southeast Asia are growing fast, but at what cost to the environment? Forests are being cut down, rivers polluted, land eroded, and cities congested with traffic. Dams to generate hydroelectric power have flooded rare habitats. Agriculture on steep slopes has increased erosion. Sediment has filled rivers, killing fish. Cars and factories release fumes

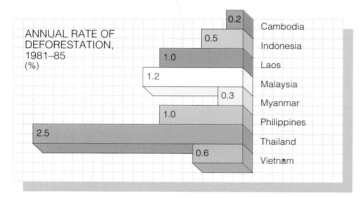

ANNUAL RATE OF DEFORESTATION, 1981–85 (%)

Country	Rate
Cambodia	0.2
Indonesia	0.5
Laos	1.0
Malaysia	1.2
Myanmar	0.3
Philippines	1.0
Thailand	2.5
Vietnam	0.6

▶ *Traffic pollution in Bangkok is so bad that police officers wear masks and sometimes take breaths of oxygen from cylinders by the side of the road.*

▼ *Tropical hardwood logs await export at Sandakan Harbor in Sabah, Malaysia. Malaysia exports $3 billion of timber a year, clearing 629,850 acres (255,000 ha) of forest.*

and pollutants, causing health problems.

Until the mid-1970s, these issues were largely ignored because poverty was a greater problem. But now that people in Southeast Asia are becoming richer, they are more concerned about the state of their countries' environment. Organizations such as Malaysia's Sahabat Alam Malaysia (Friends of the Earth Malaysia) and Indonesia's Walhi (Environmental Forum) have become influential. Tourists who come to the region to see the beautiful forests and wildlife encourage governments to protect the creatures and their habitats.

It is not just animals and plants that have suffered. Southeast Asia's tribal peoples, like the Dayaks of Borneo and the Philippines, have seen their land taken away from them to make way for large-scale plantations, mining, and the timber industry. They have found it impossible to live in their traditional ways. Only a few thousand hunter-gatherers, such as the Penan of Borneo and the Kubu of Sumatra in Indonesia, still survive.

The tropical forests of Southeast Asia are second only to those of South America in size, covering more than 780,000 square

*The orangutan, or "man of the forest,"
is found only in Malaysia and Indonesia.
Adult males weigh 220 pounds (100 kg)
and stand 5.3 feet (1.6 m) tall. At the
Bohorok Rehabilitation Center in Sumatra,
orangutans captured as babies or illegally
kept in captivity are reintroduced to the
wild.*

miles (2 million sq km). Each year 7,800
square miles (20,000 sq km) are cut down —
an area the size of New Jersey. Unlike
forests in the United States and Europe,
tropical forests cannot be replanted. They
contain too many species, and the soil
rapidly erodes after the trees are gone.
However, there are some pressures on
governments to use the forests. Timber is a
valuable export, and the land can be used to
settle poor rural people who have nowhere
else to live.

Forests are not only a source of wood.
They also provide local people with many
natural products. Insects and grubs are
gathered and fried. Roots are dug up and
cooked. Wild animals are hunted for their
meat and skins. Some tribal groups sell
forest products, such as resins, camphor (a
strong-smelling oil), and the nests of the
swift (for making bird's nest soup).

KEY FACTS

● The kouprey of Cambodia is one of the
symbols of the World Wide Fund for Nature,
but it is thought to be almost extinct.
● The world's largest lizard is the Komodo
dragon of eastern Indonesia, which can
grow up to 10 feet (3 m) in length and has
been known to kill and eat humans.
● Below Bangkok, the Chao Phraya River is
so polluted that it is biologically dead.
● In Malaysia, 176 species of trees have
been recorded in 2.5 acres (1 ha) of rain
forest.
● Indonesia loses more than 3.2 million
acres (1.3 million ha) of forest per year —
more than any other country in the world
except Brazil.

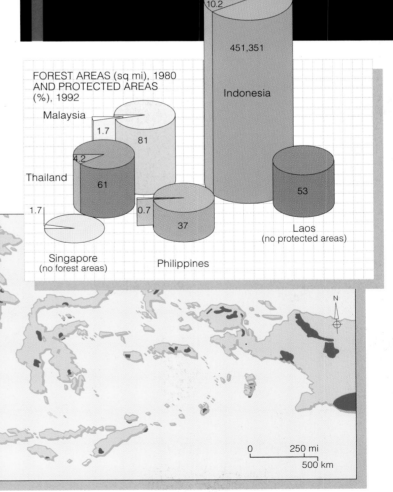

FOREST AREAS (sq mi), 1980
AND PROTECTED AREAS
(%), 1992

Malaysia

10.2

451,351

Indonesia

Malaysia
1.7
81

Thailand
4.2
61

1.7

0.7

37

53

Laos
(no protected areas)

Singapore
(no forest areas)

Philippines

THE NATIONAL PARKS
OF INDONESIA

0   250 mi

500 km

N

THE FUTURE

There is a "fast-track" and a "slow-track" Southeast Asia. Singapore, Malaysia, Thailand, and Indonesia have developed rapidly. They are classified as middle-income countries, or close to that. Brunei is a small, oil-rich country. But until very recently, Vietnam, Laos, Cambodia, the Philippines, and Myanmar have had slow-growing or stagnant economies. The future holds different prospects for each group of countries.

Signs of success among the "fast-track" countries are easy to find. For instance, Indonesia makes advanced airplanes, and in 1984 it launched the Palapa-B communications satellite. And Malaysia produces a national car. However, such successes hide problems and challenges. There is a shortage of skilled workers, and education levels are low. Development has led to environmental problems. One in five Indonesians and Thais are still classified as poor. There is a wide gap between the wealth of cities and the poverty of the countryside.

The problems of "slow-track" Southeast Asia are more challenging. These countries must develop and improve their roads, railroads, ports, banks, power stations and telecommunications. The basic elements of a modern economy are absent. Foreign companies complain about the difficulties of doing business in countries such as Vietnam, for example. But if these countries overcome such challenges, they may be confronted by the problems facing "fast-track" Southeast Asia.

KEY FACTS

● Corazón Aquino became Southeast Asia's first female leader when she was elected president of the Philippines in 1986.
● Annual population growth in Singapore, Thailand, and Indonesia was 2–2.7 percent in the 1970s. It is expected to fall to 1.4–1.5 percent by the year 2000.
● Indonesia's population is set to reach 265 million in 2025 and to peak at 354 million later in the 21st century.

A common issue across the region is the need to maintain good relations among different ethnic groups and religions. In Malaysia, for example, tension between the Chinese (who control the economy) and Malays (who dominate politics) bubbles just beneath the surface. Concern for human rights and a desire for greater democracy present both an opportunity and a danger. In May 1992, when demonstrators challenged the military government in Thailand, the army was called in, and more than 100 people were killed. But the demonstrators achieved their goals, and the government was forced to resign.

Overall, however, the future is bright. The economies of the countries in the region are growing rapidly, and their problems seem to be manageable. Southeast Asia's inhabitants are becoming wealthier, healthier, and better educated.

▶ *The first Indonesian satellite, named Palapa-B, was launched in 1984. Palapa-B provides satellite communications for the country.*

◀ *The Vietnamese government is encouraging foreign companies to invest, and many are now drilling for oil and gas in the South China Sea. Here, a foreign expert gives advice on the construction of a new oil refinery near Ho Chi Minh City.*

FURTHER INFORMATION

- BRUNEI CHANCERY
2600 Virginia Avenue NW, Washington, DC 20037
- BURMA CHANCERY
2300 South Street NW, Washington, DC 20008
- INDONESIAN TOURIST OFFICE
3457 Wilshire Boulevard, Los Angeles, CA 90010
- LAOS CHANCERY
2222 South Street NW, Washington, DC 20008
- MALAYSIAN TOURIST CENTRE
818 West 7th Street, Los Angeles, CA 90017
- PERMANENT MISSION OF CAMBODIA TO THE UNITED NATIONS
820 2nd Avenue, New York, NY 10017
- PERMANENT MISSION OF THE SOCIALIST REPUBLIC OF VIETNAM TO THE UNITED NATIONS
20 Waterside Plaza, New York, NY 10010
- PHILIPPINE DEPARTMENT OF TOURISM
3460 Wilshire Boulevard, Los Angeles, CA 90010

- SINGAPORE TOURIST BOARD
342 Madison Avenue, New York, NY 10173
- THAILAND TOURISM AUTHORITY
3440 Wilshire Boulevard, Los Angeles, CA 90010

BOOKS ABOUT SOUTHEAST ASIA

Chandler, David P. *The Land and People of Cambodia*. HarperCollins Children's, 1991

Goodman, Jim. *Thailand*. Marshall Cavendish, 1991

Layton, Lesley. *Singapore*. Marshall Cavendish, 1991

Major, John S. *The Land and People of Malaysia and Brunei*. HarperCollins Children's, 1991

Mason, Antony. *Southeast Asia*. Raintree Steck-Vaughn, 1992

McGuire, William. *Southeast Asians*. Watts, 1991

McNair, Sylvia. *Indonesia*. Childrens, 1993

Saw Myat Yin. *Burma*. Marshall Cavendish, 1991

Seah, Audrey. *Vietnam*. Marshall Cavendish, 1993

Tope, Lily R. *Philippines*. Marshall Cavendish, 1991

Zickgraf, Ralph. *Laos*. Chelsea, 1991

GLOSSARY

ANIMISM
Religions, associated with tribal peoples, based on the worship of natural objects, such as trees and mountains

CAPITALISM
An economic system where individuals own businesses and keep the profits

COLONIAL
Of a system where a country is occupied and ruled by people from a different country

COMMUNIST
Describes an economic and political system where the state controls most of the economy, and private ownership is largely abolished

CONFUCIANISM
A philosophy, religion, and way of life based on the writings of Confucius (551–479 B.C.). It stresses the importance of family and the worship of ancestors.

DAOISM
A Chinese religion and philosophy based on maintaining balance and harmony in life

ECOSYSTEM
The interactions of communities of plants and animals with their surroundings

FAULT LINES
Places where Earth's geological plates meet. They are usually prone to earthquakes and volcanic eruptions.

IRRIGATE
To supply water for cultivating crops, for example using water channels

LEMONGRASS
An aromatic plant used to spice soups and curries

MAHAYANA BUDDHISM
A form of Buddhism practiced in Vietnam

THERAVADA BUDDHISM
A form of Buddhism practiced in Thailand, Laos, Myanmar, and Cambodia, as well as Sri Lanka

TYPHOON
From the Chinese *tai fung* or "big wind;" the name given to hurricanes in the South China Sea

INDEX